Brooklin moore

This Is What Love Does

Marianne Marrone Weaver

Publisher - eGenCo

Generation Culture Transformation
Specializing in publishing for generation culture change

eGenCo
824 Tallow Hill Road
Chambersburg, PA 17202, USA
Phone: 717-461-3436
email: info@egen.co
Website: www.egen.co

facebook.com/egenbooks
youtube.com/egenpub
egen.co/blog

Publisher's Cataloging-in-Publication Data
Weaver, Marianne Marrone
This is What Love Does; by Marianne Marrone Weaver.
32 pages cm.
ISBN: 9781936554812 hardback
      9781936554829 ebook
      9781936554836 ebook
1. Religion. 2. Love. 3. Hope. I. Title
2014944272

Illustrations – Jessica Stauffer, www.jessicastauffer.com
Cover Layout and Interior Layout – Kevin Lepp, www.kmlstudio.com

First Edition Print

DEDICATION

This story is dedicated to my amazing daughters, Kristen and Tina, who inspire me daily; to my sweet brother, Vinnie, whom I am privileged to love; and to my dear friend, Lindsey, without whom Dubzee would not exist.

FOREWORD

This Is What Love Does is a story about a little girl named Dubzee who embarks on an adventure, sharing her gift of selfless love, with the hope of restoring harmony and balance within her surroundings. This story is about putting one's values into action. The reader is subtly reminded, through loving acts of kindness, that we each have the potential to create a positive impact while understanding we are all connected to something bigger. Together we are stronger. Thank you for reading.

ENDORSEMENTS

"'The Galaxy of Benevolence' is truly a place filled with valuable life lessons. Parents and children will enjoy this meaningful story, as it so relates to our day-to-day lives. Readers of all ages will find much enrichment from this wonderful tale!"

Clinton Barkdoll, Esquire

"If all parents shared this book with their children, the natural light that shines in childhood would find support, reflection, and encouragement and would very well shine on longer. Free of all negativity and cruelty, *This Is What Love Does* embraces a beautiful world where love heals and transforms and restores all to its natural state. Marianne Weaver has written a beautiful book children will love reading and listening to. She has also written a book that will allow children to feel justified in their own inherent kindness and empathy. I so love this book!"

Laura Hope-Gill
Director of the Thomas Wolfe Center for Narrative at Lenoir-Rhyne University
Poet Laureate of the Blue Ridge Parkway

"In *This Is What Love Does*, Marianne Weaver inspires children with the power of love to ignite generosity, comfort, respect, responsibility, hope, and kindness. What your children focus on is what they will CREATE! Read this tender story to your children again and again and watch the glow of goodness expand in their hearts and out to the world!"

Brian Biro
Father, Husband, Speaker, Author
America›s Breakthrough Coach

"A culture's values are kept alive though intentional efforts to pass these treasures along from one generation to the next. The best means for this exchange are role-modeling and storytelling. Marianne Weaver provides all of us a great story worthy of sharing with our loved ones. In her book, *This Is What Love Does*, she not only reminds us of timeless values, but also reawakens the wisdom of the feminine, which celebrates and courageously models the gift of caring, nurturing love. This is good medicine for all of us."

Bill Grace
Educator and Speaker
Founder of the Center for Ethical Leadership, Director of Common Good Works

COMFORT

GENEROSITY

RESPECT

KINDNESS

Once there was a Galaxy,
far, far away known as the
Galaxy of **Benevolence**.
It was a huge Galaxy made
up of many planets that
contained people and
creatures of all shapes
and sizes and colors.

HOPE

RESPONSIBILITY

There were six planets in
all! They were the planets of
**Comfort, Generosity, Respect,
Responsibility, Hope** and
Kindness.

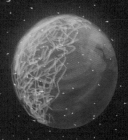

On one of those planets, the planet of **Kindness**, lived a girl named Dubzee, and she had a remarkable gift, the gift of Selfless Love.

All of the people who lived on the planets inside the Benevolent Galaxy lived their lives **demonstrating** acts of kindness to each other. They comforted their neighbors when they were sick or feeling sad. They were generous and shared what they had and they were respectful of their neighbor's property. They prided themselves on taking **responsibility** and **accountability** for their actions. They lived with the hope that they would always live in **harmony** with each other. They were proud of their Galaxy. They shouted:

We love Benevolence!!!!

Dubzee loved living on the planet of **Kindness**, in the Galaxy of **Benevolence**, with its **iridescent** purple suns and golden rivers. She loved her family, friends, and community and of course, her favorite companion, Grace, the Dragonfly!

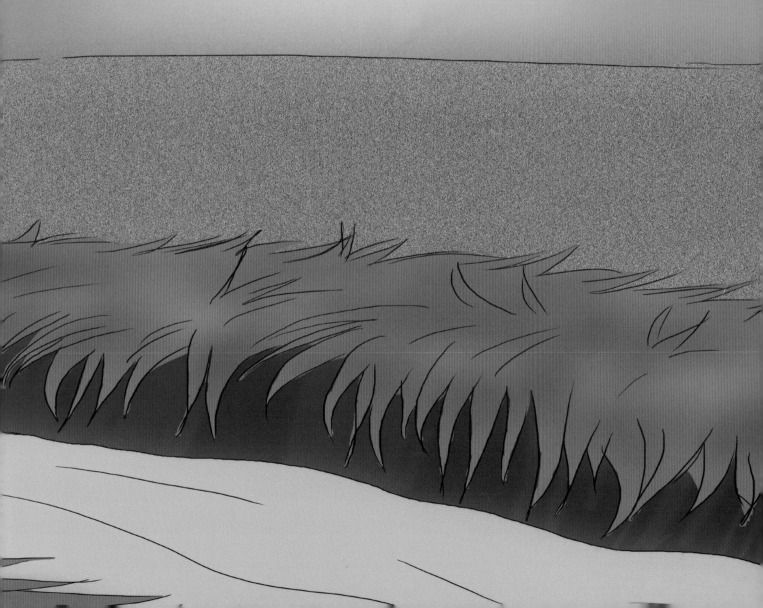

Dubzee was humble, **endearing** and hard working. Her goodness always glowed with an iridescent purple light.

She embraced her big gift and knew having it was a big responsibility. For she knew - "love won't grow unless you give it away!"

Everyone in the galaxy worked together to keep their community safe and **prosperous**.

Dubzee's assignment was to deliver the **Agape** Times to her neighbors in the Kindness neighborhoods. The newspaper was filled with wonderful stories of people, sharing and caring and cooperating with each other.

Life was good, until one day, something terrible and unexpected happened!

The headlines in the newspaper screamed. Trouble in Benevolence! Planets in Revolt!!!! No more Sharing! No Respect! NO ONE CARES!!!!

"No more comfort!" screamed the people of **Comfort**.

"No more sharing!" cried the people of **Generosity**.

"We don't need respect!" chimed in the people of **Respect**.

"Responsibility solves nothing!" cried the people of the planet **Responsibility**.

"It's hopeless!" **lamented** the people of the planet **Hope**.

AGAPE TIMES
TROUBLE IN BENEVOLENCE!
NO MORE SHARI
NO RESPECT!!!
NO ONE CARES!!!!
PLANETS IN REVOLT!!!
No Mor
Comf

The news was shocking and all the **inhabitants** of **Kindness** were saddened to hear these cruel, harsh and selfish words. At one time, everyone had worked together building **sustainable** communities, with plenty of food, water, and shelter and yes, love for each other.

As Dubzee looked up into the night sky, she felt very sad to know that the galaxy was in such **disorder** and **turmoil**.

It seemed as if all the light had gone out of the Galaxy of Benevolence! She wished that she could help make the galaxy into the loving place it had once been. But what could she do?

As she sat on a rock, sobbing, Grace brushed away Dubzee's tears. Through her tears, she could see her goodness growing dim. Now it was a faint iridescent purple glow. But she could still see it.

She listened to the soft whisper of her heart and remembered, "You must give your love away, if you want it to grow!"

She knew just what she had to do!

"We must be brave," Dubzee **exclaimed**! "We must fly to the other planets". Dubzee took flight on Grace's wings and they soared cautiously through the dimming sky.

She flew quickly to the planet of **Comfort**. She saw people pushing and shoving those who walked slowly or had an injury.

What could she do to show comfort?

Quickly, she leaned down and helped a little boy whose leg was in a cast. Others around her took note and then they followed her example by offering help to others in need. One by one, Dubzee thanked them and continued to lend a helping hand.

"What is going on here?" barked some **apathetic** onlookers, when they saw others offering to help.

"This is what love does!" shouted Dubzee.

The people of **Comfort** understood and rejoiced!

Off she went to the next planet of **Generosity**.

"Mine, it's all mine," shouted one little girl.

"No, I don't have to share," cried another little boy.

Dubzee reached down into her pocket and pulled out the last shiny gold coin she earned from her newspaper deliveries.

"Here," she said, "You take it!"

"But, isn't it yours?" the children asked.

"I want you to have it," said Dubzee.

"Why are you doing this?"

"This is what love does", said Dubzee.

Everyone instantly remembered how important it is to share.

Dubzee went quickly to the planet of **Respect**. People were pointing to each other and calling each other ugly names. They were laughing at each other. There was no respect here!

Dubzee was tempted to scold the people, but instead compassionately asked, "Would you make fun of me just because I have a purple glow?

The people put their heads down and looked embarrassed. "No Dubzee, we are ashamed of ourselves."

Suddenly the people started to hug and shake hands.

"This is what love does," said Dubzee.

They agreed that the strength of their community is *in* their differences. They remembered that each one has a unique gift and together these gifts compliment the other.

When Dubzee arrived at the planet of **Responsibility**, she noticed that all the people were getting lazy and not tending to their crops. The plants were wilted and crying out for water and attention.

She filled a watering can with cool, fresh water and began giving each plant a drink. She carefully mounded the soil around the base of each plant and patted it gently.

"Grow little plant," she cooed.

When others saw her, they humbly pitched right in and started pulling out the weeds and raking the soil into straight rows.

They laughed and talked and
stood up taller, with a sense of
dignity and **accomplishment**.

"This is good," they said smiling.

"This is what love does,"
said Dubzee.

The people remembered how
rewarding responsibility is to all of the community.

At the last planet of **Hope**, Dubzee witnessed **despair**. Everyone had their heads down and they were moaning.

"We are doomed," they said.

"Things will never get better," they all agreed.

Dubzee got right to work, spreading love in the best way she knew. She took time to listen to what people had to say with an open and compassionate heart. She led others to the community center where they volunteered to help distribute food and clothing. She gathered others and they silently spent time together holding hands **reflecting** on their blessings.

Hope was restored.

"This is what love does," said Dubzee.

The people of **Hope** waved goodbye as Dubzee and Grace flew away through the warm and beautiful violet sky.

They returned to the
planet of **Kindness** eager to deliver the Agape Times.
They noticed the colorful birds perched in the trees
and the spring like weather. The headline reads –

Benevolence Restored!!

"How did this happen?"

"This is what love does," Dubzee said beaming.

VOCABULARY DEFINITIONS

accomplishment: Something that you complete successfully. Great job when you complete something you finished! Name something that you have started and finished.

accountability: Being willing to accept responsibility for your actions and words. It is a sign of growing up. Can you remember a time that you were accountable for something you did?

agape: Great big love. Who is someone you love?

apathetic: Not really caring about something or getting excited over something. Do you think feeling apathetic feels good or bad?

benevolence: A kind act. Tell about a time you were benevolent.

comfort: To help someone feel less scared or worried. How do you like to be comforted when you are scared or worried?

demonstrating: To show how to do something. Do you have a story to share about kindness being demonstrated?

dignity: When your actions and words honor and respect yourself and others. Can you think of any way that you have shown dignity?

disorder: When things are not the way they are supposed to be. What do you think shows disorder?

despair: To not have hope that things will get better and to be very sad or worried about it. Have you ever felt despair? How did that make you feel?

endearing: To cause feelings of affection. Is anyone or anything endearing to you?

exclaim: To say or do something with excitement. What makes you excited?

generosity: Being kind and not selfish and to give your time or things to help someone else. Can you remember a time when you were generous?

harmony: Different things working together to make something great. Do you like to live in harmony?

hope: To want something to happen or be true and think that it could happen or be true. What is something you hope to happen?

inhabitant: A person or animal that lives in a particular place. Name some of the inhabitants who live on our planet Earth?

iridescent: Shining with many different colors when seen from different ways. What looks iridescent to you?

kindness: Being nice to others. Describe a time you were kind or someone was kind to you.

lamented: To express sadness. What would be a time for lamenting?

prosperous: Strong and healthy in growth. How can someone prosper?

reflect: To think deeply about a situation. Do you think it is good for people to reflect?

respect: A feeling of looking up to someone or something that is good, valuable and important and treating them like they are good, valuable and important. Who do you respect?

responsibility: A duty or task that you are required or expected to do. Do you have any responsibilities at home?

sustainable: Using something without using all of it or not destroying something so you can use it for a really long time. What can we do to sustain our environment?

turmoil : A very confused feeling. What confuses you?

Learn more about

Marianne Marrone Weaver

www.facebook.com/MarianneMarroneWeaverAuthor

Generation Culture Transformation
Specializing in publishing for generation culture change

Visit us Online at: www.egen.co

Write to: eGenCo, 824 Tallow Hill Road, Chambersburg, PA 17202 USA
Phone: 717-461-3436 | Email: info@egen.co

 facebook.com/egenbooks    youtube.com/egenpub    egen.co/blog